The Power of CONNECTION

Transformation Happens Within to Connect the Dots

Babu Nejakar

 pencil

ISBN **978-93-5458-193-9**
© Babu Nejakar 2021
Published in India 2021 by Pencil

A brand of
One Point Six Technologies Pvt. Ltd.
123, Building J2, Shram Seva Premises,
Wadala Truck Terminal, Wadala (E)
Mumbai 400037, Maharashtra, INDIA
E connect@thepencilapp.com
W www.thepencilapp.com

All rights reserved worldwide

DISCLAIMER: *The opinions expressed in this book are those of the authors and do not purport to reflect the views of the Publisher.*

Author biography

This book is written by Mr Babu Nejakar a mentor, coach, and social worker. He is working with students, people from the development sector and helping them to move forward in their journey through his thought leadership. He faced many ups and downs but his major strength is not giving up easily. He is like sthitaprajna, taking any situation in a calm state and moving forward with hope. He is friendly, caring is his core strength, supporting is his happiness, sharing his learning and life experience is his hobby.

CONTENTS

Preface

Doing Good is a simple and universal vision. A vision to which each and every one of us can connect and contribute to its realization. A vision based on the belief that by doing good deeds, positive thinking, and affirmative choice of words, feelings, and actions, we can enhance goodness in the world. -Shari Arison

Someone who unconditionally loves you cares for you, supports you, and guides you in every facet of your life becomes your hero.

Parents? Yes, they are your heroes, but still, there is someone else who without asking for anything from you wants to see you go higher and higher above in life. One who isn't jealous, but is more than happy at your success. Yes, he or she is the one that deserves this title.

A hero is one who inspires goodness in people. Someone people look up to. Not everyone can be that. A hero is not just a person, he/she is a symbol, that if you hold on tight, and not give up, you will prosper.

For me, my father is my hero. I always see signs of hard work on his face, crow's feet, wrinkles, scars. Signs of responsibility, signs of sacrifice, all for his family. And what saddens me, is that even if I try my hardest, I might not be half the man he is. Strangely, the same thing makes me proud. He is the epitome of hard work, struggle, of greatness. And he inspires me whenever I see him, to be a better person, to hold on, to not give up when it gets tough because it's all going to be alright in the end. He is that assurance to me.

Just looking at his face reminds me, that I have big shoes to fill. He sometimes scolds me when I do something wrong & nags me when I am not doing what I am supposed to. At first, I am irritated, but then I realize that under all that, he prays for me to be better, bigger, stronger than him. Just looking at him reminds me of his concern for me, which might be too much sometimes, but it is always correct. Always.

Anyone who wants to be a hero should be a dad first. They should know what it feels like to have all their strengths, and all their weakness concentrated into one living entity.

All of us want to express ourselves freely. But when you decide to look tough outside even when your whole universe is crumbling inside you, to fake that smile, so it inspires others to do the same. To teach someone how to live. Not many people can do that. I love my Dad because he does just this. He is my hero, every single day, for my whole life.

The conversation mentioned sounds cool and inspired? then the same hero is there in every human being. We need to find the hero within ourselves and need to nurture the hero to become a superhero.

Acknowledgements

I acknowledge and appreciate every friend and family members who contributed, encouraged and support to writing this book, I am dedicating this book to all of them.

Section-1 Connect to the Inner World

Chapter -1 The Beauty of Inner World

"It is still breathtaking to me to watch people bring love, preciousness, and kindness to their inner world, allowing the light of God to shine through their eyes so that the beauty of their soul can come forth" -Debbie Ford

We always experience the two worlds, one is the inner world that is within us and the outer world that is around us. we always stand in the middle and try to connect both worlds to experience the essence of life.

Everything created twice by us, the first version in the inner world and the second version in the outer world. So if we want the best creation in the outer world, we need to create the best in the inner world. If we want happiness then first we need to experience the happiness within us. If we want wealth in life then we need to experience the same wealth within us first.

likewise, anything we want in our life, consciously we need to create the same thing first in the inner world. Otherwise, the result in the outer world will go by default and sure we will not happy with the default result.

When I thought beauty inner world always went to my tiny happy childhood. I was born and brought up in a very small village, mud roads, away from the main road, the bull cart is the primary source for travel, chill in winter, heavy rain in the rainy season, heavy hot in summer.

Now I am 41year old I am able to recollect my memory from the 1st standard of my government school education so 33years back from now was like that I feel internal, over the period the things are changed, the feelings are changed but the connection with the journey is not changed.

What are the things you most enjoy in the world around you? Mountains? Ocean? Skies filled with clouds? A happy gathering of friends or family? Those are some of the things that suggest themselves to me as a beautiful outer world.

So take those same things inside yourself - are you happy alone? Can you amuse yourself without the need for others to be around? Do your favorite books "come alive" to you when you read them?

We live inside of the world of thoughts and impressions - a beautiful inner world is one where those thoughts and impressions are sufficient to make us happy and satisfied

Well, that would involve all the intangibles like thoughts, ideas, feelings, intuition, imagination, hopes, fears, etc.

Basically, it is said of a person who is a creative thinker with a parallel world constructed inside his/her head. It's a private space which is yours alone. To do with as you like. One could liken it to a study desk, a garden, a cemetery, a prayer house, a fantasy land, a place of possibilities.

It could also involve retrospection, introspection, visualization, meditation or holding intentions, illusions, and fantasy.

The beautiful inner world is not separate from the outer world and includes the essential connectivity with relationships of life, simultaneously.

There are four essential relationships valid at any time, place, circumstance. Richness expands without limit for those who meld their uniqueness, with the every-where, when, what.

The totality is us, and we are it, and every being is an aspect, and unique.

When the artificial distinctions drop away, the beautiful richness of any moment, any time, anywhere can be perceived.

You are in tune with your emotions and what triggers them.

You are accepting of all your imperfections and don't beat yourself up when you goof up.

You are accepting and understanding of other people and their reality and allow them to be who they are.

There are way more things, but you get the message.

You would be fun to be around, a joy to talk and listen to, and would put people at ease so as to decrease the chance for argument or defense mechanisms to kick in.

Happiness is a decision. You can even buy Happiness. But with Joy, you need conscious effort to make it your conviction to be. By accepting truths. Your Truth. Truths that you build and discover for yourself.

The body and mind become separate, and you no longer need to think to do things; you just do them. This is "enlightenment" as people call it, but in reality, accessing this inner world, this inner power, and understanding, is just the beginning of a long process of growth so go-ahead to connect with both the worlds.

Chapter -2 Travel Around the Inner world

Travel can be one of the most rewarding forms of introspection- Lawrence Durrell

If we look into the inner world clearly as it can look far more interesting as it envelops any environment in the Universe the ability to reach this space is effortless The beauty of the Inner world is abundant with beauty, peace, joy and there is no fear, no threats no division of status its as pure and transparent as crystal.

In the outer world, You can be a friend, brother/sister, employee, boyfriend/girlfriend, husband/wife, partner, father/mother, son/daughter, all at the same time, but these are just an aspect of you. They don't represent who you fundamentally are inside. Your inner self is who you really are on the inside.

Knowing your inner self requires a high level of introspection and self-awareness. If you have the clarity to at least half of what is listed above, you probably hold quite a high level of self-awareness. At the same time, the process of discovery never ends – it's a life-long journey.

Trying to uncover your inner self can be a tricky process. For one, you hold multiple identities in your life, each with its own sets of socially defined values, visions, expectations, etc. These may not directly conform to what you represent.

It is common for people to see themselves as a certain role, such as a friend, partner, employee, son/daughter, and so on. Some spend their whole lives building themselves around such identities. Take those identities away, and they get totally lost because they have a low awareness of who they are on the inside. These people are not able to articulate his/her own visions, goals, and dreams beyond what has been imposed by his/her identities.

For example, someone who is entrenched in his identity as a son will see his entire existence as a son. He will act in accordance with what's best for his parents. He will spend a lot of time with his parents, do things for his parents, forsake other things in his life if it's needed to make them happy. When it comes to making important decisions, such as a career or life partner, he makes sure his parents are in approval before he takes any action. His parents are the central focus of his life.

However, his real self is more than just being a son to his parents. If his parents are to ever exit from his life, he will be in a state of a total loss. His life will start spiraling out of control since the anchor he has been building his life on so far is gone. It's like when the bulb of the sunflower disappears, all the petals will scatter away randomly since there is nothing to hold them together. When you become overly attached to any one of your identities, you run into the risk of an identity crisis when that particular identity is removed.

This life is one that's defined by you, not what is defined by your roles or identities. If you are not connected with who you really are, you are probably just living your life for others. Pursuing others' goals, living up to others' expectations and projections of you, rather than what you really want.

For example, if you find yourself often extolling on being responsible to your parents, responsibility is likely one of your inner values. If you feel a compelling need to always be there for your friends, reliability is probably an important value to you.

What others see as you are the physical you. You can see some people are calm and happy even when they are working very hard and struggling in life. Others will feel that they are totally dissatisfied and life is very difficult for them. But they are doing everything with a smile and enjoy every bit of life. You can also see people who are rich - worldly rich - but still dissatisfied. They always want more and more. It is because their inner life is not satisfying and wanted to earn more and more. However or whatever they earn they will not be happy. They may present themselves in public as very happy and satisfied. But their actions expose their real nature.

The inner world is how you feel about yourself and others. Outer life is how you present yourself to others, or how others see you. So always travel around your inner world and experince the things around your inner world.

Chapter-3 Play and Enjoy the game within you

Life is a song - sing it. Life is a game -play it. Life is a challenge - meet it. Life is a dream - realize it. Life is a sacrifice - offer it. Life is love - enjoy it -Sai Baba

When we ignore the higher-level purpose of life, we see everything as meaningless; that feeling increases anxiety and depression. Regardless of how successful we are with our personal objectives, we may not feel secured without addressing the high-level objective; the purpose of our existence.

Our life on earth is a very short period compared to the universe time scale; It could be a temporary test period. God is testing us in our short life on earth; the wealthy father has the right to test his children before distributing the wealth. he tests us and wants us to witness our own test results in order to admit that we have been fairly rewarded according to our achievements as recorded in the test results

Testing missions are not supposed to be easy and comfortable. The test questions are not supposed to be known in advance. Our life on earth is a very short period compared to the universe time scale; It could be a temporary test period.

Before the wealthy father distributes his wealth, he may want to record which son is obedient, the records are not for the father who knows, but as a testimony for people who might question the justice of their father

Although the wise teacher knows the hard-working student and the lazy student, he prepares regular exams as testimonies so that the students would not say that the teacher had favored some students over the others. Exams also urge students to get prepared in order to succeed We have not created the gifts of sight, intelligence, conscience, and many other gifts.

You might not realize but we all are playing this console game called life whose remote controller is our brain. There are various levels in the game and you have to finish each level to progress to the next level. We can move from level 1 to level 2, but we cannot move directly from level 1 to level 10 unless you find some cheat codes.

You can use *cheat codes* like *fraud, bribery, scam,* etc which will get you penalized if you get caught by the *Game Admin.* Another way is using abstract elements and working hard to acquire new skills and assets. Though this will take time and will require patience and persistence. And you might not get a whole lot of resources to complete this level. But you'll have to realize, the main purpose of this game is to enjoy it, rather than win it.

The game starts when you were born. You are assigned a character. Unfortunately, you have no choice over the traits of this character like physical appearance and mental abilities. His strengths and weaknesses are genetically hard-coded and you cannot change them for now. But you can work upon them later in life.

At the start of the game, you had no control over who you were or your environment. By the end of the game that becomes true again. Your past decisions drastically shape where you end up, and if you're happy, healthy, fulfilled – or not – in your final days there's far less you can do about it. That's why your strategy is important.

There are many facets to this game and many realities, but there is no doubt that life is one huge game. Here are a few realities that determine who gets ahead in this game called life.

- Reality 1: good-looking people have an advantage

- Reality 2: if you're not good-looking you can still earn an advantage if you're smart/ambitious.

- Reality 3: if you're neither good-looking nor smart/ambitious there is still a place for you in life. You can be a pawn or a statistic. A pawn is basically a filler piece, we need people to work as cashiers at gas stations or McDonald's, or the supermarket. A statistic is a piece that fills a necessary and inevitable percentage of the population that will "fail". These people are on welfare, food stamps, or other government-funded assistance which good-looking and smart/ambitious people provide through paying taxes.

- Reality 4: it's not what you know, it's who you know. People who succeed know other people who succeed. They also use these connections to achieve their goals. The player with the most connections is the player who wins/gets that coveted promotion.

- Reality 5: life does not hand you opportunities. You have to chase and get these opportunities. In other words, if you want that promotion, instead of trying to silently make yourself shine, you need to ask for the promotion and clearly state why you deserve it. Repeat as needed.

- Reality 6: manipulators are not evil, manipulators are winners. Which brand name will you choose when you go shoe shopping? Whichever brand was successful in imprinting their brand name on your brain in the most discreet yet effective way possible. So what is the brand name in this scenario? The brand name is you, and the brain is other people. Human beings are the keys and obstacles in life. The most successful players are the ones which can most effectively turn the keys and move the obstacles.

- Reality 7: worrying will not make you safer. A certain percentage of people will die because of fluke accidents. Worrying about this percentage will not make you safer or happier. You are not special, entitled to safe passage through life, or even less likely to die because an airplane fell on your car. You are simply a member of a population. You are exposed to the same risks, and you are just as likely to become a statistic as everyone else. The sooner you stop spending energy on useless worrying, the sooner you can be using that energy on other facets of the game.

- Reality 8: successful people learn from successful people. If you want to learn about success, the most effective way is to hear a lot of advice from a lot of people who have succeeded already

So time is precious, the only way you can fail is if you never begin. If you want to do something, do it now! Don't waste your time.

Chapter-4 Inner connection of mind and body

Your time is limited, so don't waste it living someone else's life. Don't be trapped by dogma - which is living with the results of other people's thinking. Don't let the noise of others' opinions drown out your own inner voice. And most important, have the courage to follow your heart and intuition. -Steve Jobs

A story we heard:

In an old city in the ancient era, there once lived a prostitute and a monk. They didn't know each other. They weren't even acquaintances. Yet each Of them was deeply influenced by the other. Their lives were closely connected.

Every evening as the prostitute left her home on the way to earning a night's wage she would pass by the Buddhist temple where this monk lived, And every evening the young monk would be seated outside in the temple garden doing meditation. As the young prostitute passed by the temple she would see the monk seated in meditation and would think to herself, "What an amazing young man. What a noble life he is leading. Such a pure existence, untainted by the worries andconcerns of this world. How rare and how wonderful!"

These thoughts sustained the young woman and gave her the strength to endure her life. Just to know that someone was leading such a pure life gave her both hope andencouragement, even though she knew that such purity could never be her own. She always felt blessed just walking by the temple andbeing in the presence of such sacred energy.

The monk, although supposedly seated in deep meditation couldn't help but notice the woman as well. Every evening as the young woman passed by the temple, the monk would become distracted and think to himself, "What an immoral woman. How could she make a living doing what she does? Selling her body, how low can a person go! Where are her self-respect and dignity?! What a wasted life. She would be better off dead!"

This story points out the consequences ofour inner-motivations and self-talk, Inner self-talk has the power to turn a monk into a prostitute and a prostitute into a monk.

The monk lost all peace-of-mind in the presence of the young woman, while the young woman experienced a peace of mind she never thought possible while in the presence of the monk.

Although the monk andthe prostitute were powerful influences in each other's lives, where was the real power coming from? What was the true source of both the monk's turmoil and the woman's peace-of-mind? In each case, it was their inner self-talk that was at the core of the matter.

The young woman's inner-talk was pure and selfless in the presence of the monk. The monk's inner-talk was soiled and deeply disturbed in the presence of the woman. And each experienced the immediate consequences of the kind of self-talk they entertained. The woman became very peaceful, and the monk became very disturbed.

So, there is a very strong connection between the body and mind. the great philosopher Earl Nightingale said, "What's going on in the inside shows on the outside".

Chapter-5 Nurture the inner sense

Nurture your minds with great thoughts. To believe in the heroic makes heroes. -Benjamin Disraeli

Nurturing our inner senses is the magical way to enjoy our life through connect fully with this universe. Our senses are the doors to connects us to this universe and we feel and experience the aliveness of life only through this connection. so for a tiny happy life consciously we need to nurture the connections.

To nurture your body I believe you must breathe, drink, eat, sleep, clothe and shelter it, in that order. Exercise, getting outside, seeing beautiful things and places, reading, conversation, exploration, all of these are great for your body and brain.

To nurture your inner world you need stillness. It is silence, a profound listening, an inner sense that detected the most subtle movements and energies, thoughts reactions, and impulses. Stillness is an awareness of the inner world and consequently, the cleansing and healing of it, so that you may take it back as your kingdom, your self.

Your inner world needs attending, the body needs very little, yet we give it too much attention. It does better by itself, without us manipulating it to fit our ideas of beauty.

As said your inner world needs stillness as urgently as your body needs breath. Stillness is a thickening of time, a slowing down of movement, a decrease of activity, a step sideways, not a step forward. Perhaps you can feel the silence of the mind when you choose to be aware instead of choosing to think.

Stillness shows you things the mind doesn't want you to see.

Stillness shows you secrets ego is hiding from you.

Stillness invites choice where slavery to reaction lived just yesterday.

Stillness invites wisdom to enter where a false sense of knowledge lived just moments ago.

Stillness is peace.

Stillness is you, yourself, your soul and spirit, your home, your kingdom within, your path to God or Faith.

Life is like a rail journey connected with two equal tracks of Inner world and Outer world. So need to take it easy with conscious choices:

- Keep moving. Even if you have to crawl.
- Know when to quit. It's okay to try and fail.
- Know when to take risks. Not everything is worth it.
- Know when to speak. Silence is a great language.
- Patience is the key to success. Some things take longer to happen.
- Even if you don't believe in anything, believe in your thoughts.
- Don't curse your day before it ends. Some things happen in the eleventh hour.
- Every pain helps you grow.
- Anger blurs your vision. Happiness improves your

sight.
- When disappointment comes, keep believing.
- Nobody ever got better overnight.
- Don't be deterred by your enemies. They wouldn't hurt you if they knew who you were.
- Teachers only teach you theory, but it is the struggles of life that educate you.
- Don't overlook little things. Maybe they're the only things you're required to look at.
- Don't carry over today's troubles forward
- Always do your best no matter how discouraged you feel.
- Don't do it because it's convenient. Do it because it's a commitment.
- Never lose focus on your dream even if nobody seems to care.
- When nobody seems to care, dance to your own song.
- Don't spend too much energy giving thought to problems.
- Always ignore your erratic mind and allow the inner voice to guide you.

So we need to experience the saying by Alfred Austin "The glory of gardening: hands in the dirt, head in the sun, heart with nature. To nurture a garden is to feed not just on the body, but the soul".

Chapter- 6 Inner Authentic Self

I wake up and play a different person every day. Playing all these different characters and trying to figure out who your true authentic self is at the core of that as you're playing all these different roles, and man, that self-awareness starts to come into effect. And you start to see who you really are. - Eliza Dushku

First, you need to know yourself, specifically to know your purpose, vision, values, passions, talents, and intuition. The next is to trust and believe all of these things. After that to live them all without fear or compromise in all situations. The last is really a lifelong journey as you gradually learn how to stay true to yourself in more and more and tougher situations.

In terms of authentic self-expression you probably already do this when relaxed, with people you trust, and where there is no agenda. By going through the process above you can expand the circle of people with whom you can be authentic. There will always be times, people, and situations that catch you out and those are the situations where you can learn and step up to the next level.

Authentic people:

- Are true to themselves. They are reliable, honest, and trustworthy. They "talk the talk" and "walk the walk.

- They don't live to impress people. They treat everyone with kindness and respect. They are consistent with their behavior whether they know the person or they don't.

- They are emotionally intelligent and self-aware. They give much thought to their behavior and understand how it can influence others.

- They seek genuine connections with others. They are fully present and attentive in their conversations. They not easily distracted.

- They are good listeners and seek to understand.

- They are open-minded with their thinking and the people around them. They are willing to hear various opinions and will consider- without bias- new ideas and new ways of doing things.

- They don't return unkind behavior directed towards them, they instead choose to take the high road.

Normally we are all authentic by born. but how do we lose it? Much depends on seeing our connection in the eyes of others. We limit our sense of self to how significant others have related to us as we are learning our way into the world. If our sense of self is limited to those connections, we lose sight of our own authentic self, who we are without words.

Why some time people are unable to be authentic?

Because we're so messed up, that it would get in the way of all our necessary social interactions.

Why my coworkers care about my passions or insecurities. why my neighbors care about my crazy dream I had. Nobody, except for a few people who I really matter to the most. So choosing to hide, to keep all my innermost thoughts and the craziness of my mind safely tucked away, is something I do to avoid scaring people. Because people have their own minds to scare themselves with, and their own craziness to control. And likewise, if I had to worry about everyone's disgusting little secrets, I'd get sick of people way faster than I already do.

If you don't believe me yet, look at all your darkest secrets, your deepest fears, and think how confused, traumatized, lost, and scared you would be if you knew all that stuff about everyone you met. That's why people are unable to be authentic.

So the word authenticity is the state of something being authentic, or true. Authenticity is important when the value of something is dependent on where it came from or how it was made.

The Authentic Self may look like this:

-Someone who talks more about the success of others than the success of themselves.

-Someone that listens before speaking.
-Someone that thinks before they act.
-Someone willing to take responsibility.
-Someone with nothing to prove.
-Someone that uses few words.

So, being inner authentic to yourself means you are in touch with your emotions, no suppressing, no hiding, no running away. When you're sad, you cry and if someone asks you, you express your sadness without fear of being vulnerable or show your weakness. Your face looks gloomy, your body is heavy and people can tell in your tone of voice. When you are happy, your eyes show, your smile shows, your whole face and body show.

You accept your insecurities and incompetence but you also accept that you are unique and you have the power to change your life. You know that you are living for yourself, by your rules and you are responsible for your actions and behaviors, you don't need anyone's validation and acceptance. It doesn't mean you don't respect and care about others. You're not trying to fit in somewhere that you don't belong. You have purpose and direction and you know your strengths and weaknesses that's all.

Chapter- 7 Inner Self-mastery

No matter what kind of challenges or difficulties or painful situations you go through in your life, we all have something deep within us that we can reach down and find the inner strength to get through them. -Alana Stewart

We make thousands of decisions a day, and up to 90% of them are made on a subconscious level, so it seems that developing your inner-self is important.

The greats of this world have chased after a way to develop their inner-self from the moment they believed they were dreamers at heart. It is the intensity of your desire to fulfill your inner-self that is the driving force that will help you achieve and improve your life.

Do you want your existence to be more fulfilled? Do you get up in the morning with a hunger for living, a feeling that you have perhaps forgotten since you were a child?

Then developing your inner-self will allow you to make your mark on the world because by desiring it so deeply, you will be working on it and it could truly make a difference for you and for the world around you.

It will change you forever and it will leave you with the power of being able to shape your own destiny.

What Happens when mastering Your Inner-Self

1. Mindset -Your mindset will change and you start to hang out around different types of people and think differently.

2. Confidence -You build more self-confidence in yourself and your abilities.

3. Motivation - You get exceptionally motivated because you realize you can really do what you desire and love.

4. Positivity - You become more positive, and so, more positive things happen to you in return. It is the law of attraction.

5. Respect - You develop and grow additional mental abilities to respect yourself and others in the process.

6. Value - You value yourself even more as you are your most prized possession.

7. Problem-solving -You get better at problem-solving and toward issues that others find difficult to solve.

8. Moving on - You do make mistakes, but learn from them quickly and move on.

9. Inspiration -You get inspired and your creativity opens new ranges of possibilities

10. Gratitude -You start becoming more and more grateful for what you have and what comes your way.

Your inner-self is something that can be developed by learning new ways of thought and re-structuring it. These actions inform attitudes that in turn, and over time, change the way you behave and feel.

We need to be honest with ourselves and discover our strengths and weaknesses. Accepting these are very important. Change or improvement can be done in behaviors only when we accept that we require it. This need has to come from within.

Having discovered and come to terms with our strengths and weaknesses, we are able to then analyze why we behave in a certain manner. It is not possible to change ourselves completely, but we can control our emotions by practice, which leads us to become the master of our emotions.

For example, if you are short-tempered and tend to react immediately to situations, it is a good practice to move away from the situation immediately and perhaps write down your response or reactions. Let the emotions out not on the person you feel, but on a sheet of paper. When you feel calm, take out the paper and read what you have written. Most likely, you may even smile or laugh at yourself. This helps in controlling a strong behavior. Over time, you may come up with various other means to control emotions.

Recognition of emotional peaks and valleys is key and knowing yourself, your strengths and weaknesses, is primary.

Realistically approaching your goals and objectively analyzing yourself against them. Too often we allow ourselves to drift from what's important to achieve those goals that by the time we realize it, an emotional crash is impending. Things are rarely as great as they seem. Conversely, rarely as horrific either. There are exceptions, and emotions are allowed. Life is a rollercoaster ride, leave your emotions at the platform, however. They'll be there when you get back.

Before you master your Inner Self first you have to know that who you are? You have to know yourself before mastering it.

If you identify yourself with your external then you are in illusion because external always change. According to Science human body cells, tissues and other matter completely changes in less than 7 years and we all have experienced it also.

Now it gives a conclusion that we are not this external we are eternal souls. So if you make decisions that are eternal and based on the welfare of others then you can master your inner self.

Chapter - 8 Inner Stories

I write because something inner and unconscious forces me to. That is the first compulsion. The second is one of ethical and moral duty. I feel responsible to tell stories that inspire readers to consider more deeply who they are. - David Guterson

In June 2017, I diagnosed with a critical illness, when I heard it from the doctor literally I was not seen anything in front of me, It was completely dark some time don't know what happened to me at that time. After some time slowly start to see things around me I was in an empty room at the hospital beside my friend sitting with me. I was literally shivering, sweating, and internally cried like anything.

At that time I was a 7month old father, I mean I was enjoying the fatherhood journey with my 7-month-old baby. My heart, my mind, and my phone filled with her har smile, her laughing, her crying, her crawling, her sleeping everything of her day to day activities. but that time I have seen THE END of my story.

At that time what was my option need to go through surgery and further treatment, Doctor said after that you may speak or may not. In this junction, internally I only decided to survive at least the next 50 years for support to my child and my family in whatever the condition occur to me and decided to build inner calmness. when I was decided to leave with a stated purpose, internally I started to enjoy every movement of life and my body started to respond magically to the treatment and I came out from the fear of death and I decided to never think about death it will come one day, so need to focus on build calmness internally and work every movement towards my purpose of life.

If we consciously concentrate more on nurturing the inner world deeply, then slowly the negative inner stories will disappear and stories with possibilities will appear in front of the picture.

While your head can help you make the most rational decisions, happiness is where the inner world is. When you try to look for your life's purpose from your inner world, you naturally look for things that evoke passion and joy and find a purpose that is worth living for.

Purpose gives you a constant sense of fulfillment and achievement. When you live purposefully, you live every single moment in absolute joy and give it your best, no matter what it brings. This can only happen when you embrace life as it comes with all its risks, challenges, and newness, and stop resisting anything about it. When you feel connected with every aspect of life and are in complete alignment with it, your purpose gets fulfilled on its own.

When we feel grateful for our blessings, we are able to observe how others are working to making our lives better.

In this way, we also tend to contribute to the world beyond us and live a life of purpose. Cultivating gratitude is thus an excellent way to live a purposeful life.

Bring deep breathing and meditation into daily practice so that you are more conscious and connected with your inner-self. This connection will help you to find answers to who you are, what is your purpose, and the actions that you should take to fulfill this purpose.

So, Kim Weston beautifully said"It doesn't matter what you do, as long as you're fulfilling that inner need, and for me the need is more the process than the finished product. My photographs are stories of the process".

Chapter-9 Dating with Your Inner self

When you love yourself and are able to indulge in yourself, and you're grounded in your 'yes' or 'no,' it's nothing to ask a guy on a date. -Karrueche Tran

Dating with Inner Self or Your self is a very unique process to understand yourself and enjoy your own company. Normally dating is to go out from the crowd and enjoy the company with another person. But here we are exploring the journey of dating with your own self-company.

I always want to ride my bike alone to the long-distance and in between have tea, snacks, lunch at roadway restaurants (Dhabhas) myself alone and sometime between the journey turn my bike to the countryside villages and some time into the roadside forestry mud roads and find some silent place and simply sit and listen to my favorite music. If nobody is there in the house I enjoy grabbing my favorite book to read.

Dating yourself might include everything and anything from checking out a new place, seeing a movie, attending a book mall, etc. It might also include writing a gratitude note to yourself, journaling, treating yourself to a massage, or cooking yourself a delicious dinner with the recipe you have been wanting to try. The point is to confidently embark on the journey of doing what you love and what brings you happiness without waiting for anyone to do it with you or for you.

It id one of the best ways to nurture ourselves is to plan a nice little date. yes, alone. Here are six reasons to consider taking yourself out on a date.

1. Freedom! When you take a date for yourself the first benefit is you have the freedom to do whatever you want to do! You do not have to make concessions for anyone else. It feels good to simply let a day or night, now and again, be all about you and your tastes. It reminds you of who you are, what you love, and that you can, in fact, feel fantastic all on your own.

2. You can take your time. The greatest thing about dates with yourself is that you can take your sweet time. There is no agenda. No one is rushing you to be somewhere. You can have a plan or you can just relax and fly by the seat of your pants on your date. It is ok to slow things down and enjoy the smaller pleasures of life.

3. Independence. To be able to feel self-satisfied on your own is important to your sense of self-worth and independence. To be able to go out in public and have yourself a little date shows a level of self-comfort and satisfaction. It is important for you to remember that you are more than ok all on your own. A certain amount of time alone is exciting, relieving, and nurturing to your soul.

4. It makes you more interesting. People who can never make a decision on a date or who always speak in "we" terms can annoy the other because there is no "self" there. When you spend a certain amount of time alone it keeps you on your toes in developing your own opinions, preferences, and memories. Knowing what you want is sexy because it makes you interesting.

5. Get over your fear of being alone. The more you practice entertaining, nurturing, and dating yourself, the you learn more about what you want from your spouse. Since you're married, it is always great to reconnect with yourself and to give yourself all the things that maybe you feel you are missing from your spouse. It is about being whole all unto yourself. It is attractive to be someone who is ok being alone. When you date yourself you are not alone anyway. You are not by yourself you are with yourself.

Buddha said, "You can search throughout the entire universe for someone who is more deserving of your love and affection than you are yourself, and that person is not to be found anywhere. You yourself, as much as anybody in the entire universe deserve your love and affection."

Chapter -10 Always Connect to the Hero within You

Doing Good is a simple and universal vision. A vision to which each and every one of us can connect and contribute to its realization. A vision based on the belief that by doing good deeds, positive thinking, and affirmative choice of words, feelings, and actions, we can enhance goodness in the world. -Shari Arison

Someone who unconditionally loves you cares for you, supports you and guids you in every facet of your life becomes your hero.

Parents ? Yes they are your heroes, but still their is someone else who without asking for anything from you wants to see you go higher and higher above in life. One who isn't jealous, but is more than happy at your success. Yes he or she is the one that deserves this title.

A hero is one who inspires goodness in people. Someone people look up to. Not everyone can be that. A hero is not just a person, he/she is a symbol, that if you hold on tight, and not give up, you will prosper.

For me, my father is my hero. I always see signs of hard work on his face, crow's feet, wrinkles, scars. Signs of responsibility, signs of sacrifice, all for his family. And what saddens me, is that even if I try my hardest, I might not be half the man he is. Strangely, the same thing makes me proud. He is an epitome of hard-work, of struggle, of greatness. And he inspires me whenever I see him, to be a better person, to hold on, to not give up when it gets tough, because it's all going to be alright in the end. He is that assurance to me.

Just looking at his face reminds me, that I have big shoes to fill. He sometimes scolds me when I do something wrong & nags me when I am not doing what I am supposed to. At first I am irritated, but then I realise that under all that, he prays for me to be better, bigger, stronger than him. Just looking at him reminds me of his concern for me, which might be too much sometimes, but it is always correct. Always.

Anyone who wants to be a hero, should be a dad first. They should know what it feels like to have all their strengths, and all their weakness concentrated into one living entity.

All of us want to express ourselves freely. But when you decide to look tough outside even when your whole universe is crumbling inside you, to fake that smile, so it inspires others to do the same. To teach someone how to live. Not many people can do that. I love my Dad, because he does just this. He is my hero, every single day, for my whole life.

The conversation mentioned is sounds cool and inspired? then the same hero is there in every human being. We need to find the hero within ourself and need to nurture the hero to become super hero.

Section-2 Connect to the Outer World

Chapter -11 Connect yourself with Nature

The more aware of your intentions and your experiences you become, the more you will be able to connect the two, and the more you will be able to create the experiences of your life consciously. This is the development of mastery. It is the creation of authentic power. -Gary Zukav

Connected with nature, realize that, we're not separated from nature. we're part and parcel of the whole. The air we breathe, the water we drink, the food, the fruits, and the vegetables we consume, the beautiful sky, the flowers, and the sounds of birds, etc. Take these into deep thoughts and appreciate their essence. Feel connected.

We need to take some time out alone to be with Nature. Go to the beach, riverside, or forest, internally practice appreciate to the beauty of nature. We're already connected to Nature. It's a matter of realization.

Simply want to connect with nature? do the simple things mentioned below to connect powerfully:

1. The simplest, of course, is to walk barefoot on grass, early in the morning.

2. If you like and want to get your hands dirty, go for gardening, it's one of the biggest stress relievers in the world.

3. You can also try hugging a tree, it is again a great way to relax.

4. Sometimes, just lie down on the grass, with your eyes closed, fall asleep if you can.

5. Additionally, depending on your interests, you can also go on treks to lesser-known places.

Take small vacations and go to the least popular places, it's such an amazing experience to be alone with nature. Sounds of birds chirping, probably a small stream flowing by and the scents of wet earth and blooming flowers, etc Pure bliss!!!

If we are conscious and open to learning from nature we can relate or connect with nature like mentioned below:

Water that flows through the mountains/rivers/seas has immense power. Water is shapeless and takes any form. It can irritate the soil to give life or also damage the ecosystem if not channelized. Human nature must be like water. Formless and shapeless means a human must be flexible enough to adapt to any situation of life to be actually powerful.

Everything in nature whether it be trees, insects, plants, animals is here to give/add value to the functioning of the universe. Humans must be selfless and must have a "giving" nature. Humans must try to nurture and add value to the lives of others. Nature will anyways force you to give. Better it is to start "giving" on your own. Next time you meet anybody ask, "What can I do for you"?

There is very unique learning from "Chinese Bamboo Tree". The seed of this tree doesn't grow much for 5 years even if nurtured with all efforts. But in the sixth year itself, it grows to several feet long. For humans, this is correlated as in every 5 years one can change his / her life. If you are choosing a new path, it will take 5 years for you to persevere without seeing any growth. But you will do really well later if you can just survive for just 5 years on the same path.

Ants, Honey Bees, Lions, Elephants, etc all live in groups and are much more powerful than solo hunters and live joyfully. Humans who live in groups are much more effective, productive, and happy in life.

Everything in nature is time-bound and disciplined. There are a time and direction for the sun to rise and set time for birds to start their day and end, and several other examples. Humans must try to be disciplined in life, wake up early and sleep on time.

Chapter-12 Connect through Eyes

Connecting with people in person is so important. To look in the eyes of our girls and let them know that you really do support them transcends the impersonal connection of technology. - Grace Gealey

In 2015, I was in a training program called Self-Expression and Leadership Program by Landmark Worldwide. there is an activity to connect with the opposite person through eyes and the rule choose a person next sitting to you. I have the choice to choose a person sitting on my right side. the person is a lady around 45years of age. another rule was to keep connecting with the person without blinking the eyes even though the eyes with tears or dry with pain.

We were stand up looking at each other start to see each other in the eyes. we are the opposite gender, at the beginning, I was not comfortable at all seeing her eyes but the rule reminds me at any cost don't no distraction from the connection. In beginning, I was laughing but the lady was smiling, Internally I was shaking, many different thoughts came into my mind and after some time slowly the internal disturbance come down and connected deep in the eyes....,

The connection goes on.. goes on... and her eyes start to drop tears continuously and we were silent, body stilled with the connection. She was connected so deep into my eyes, I was distracted internally but allow her to connect with my eyes deeply so I did not distract my connection with her eyes.

It was such a powerful exercise, we were not speaking a word to each other but the connection between us went so deep and created oneness among us. we were literally felt oneness beyond our gender and everything. So, I realized from this simple and powerful exercise, human beings need connections and it is so wonderful if we connect through eyes.

Chapter- 13 Connect with Family Members

"For me, I saw a psychologist because I wanted to connect more with people, with the earth, my environment. I want to connect more to my family". -Metta World Peace

We were created for connection, it is essential to our well-being and growth. Life gives us joys along the way and having a family to share our joys and challenges in life makes them more fun and also provides valuable support during the hard times. Through the connections with family, we have discovered qualities we see in our family.

Family is our safe place to be who we are knowing we are loved and accepted for just who we are and that is important in forming our self-love and balance who we are.

As human beings, we are blessed with the awareness of our connections, and the creative capacity to define our connections.

What kind of connections do we want to have? It could be

a connection with a smartphone. It could be a connection with a type of animal. It could be a connection with another human being who also has the creative capacity to add an infinite amount of joy to our relationship.

Family and friends, as compared to strangers and enemies, are the connections that are concerned about our well-being and our happiness. Those are the quality connections that we want to build.

If we want to be part of a good quality connection, we have to be able to play our part; to care for the other and act on that care. Then others would naturally recognize us as a plus and would want to care for us. So need to care for our family and friends, because they need us, just as we need them.

I saw a beautiful story somewhere from Gurmeet Bishno, It is such a wonderful story on how connectivity is important to enjoy our happy family life. The story is herein below:

Ashok was enjoying his retired life with his wife very happy.

All three of his sons were doing jobs and living with their families in different cities. They had kept the rules that all three sons used to come to their parents on Diwali.

One day Ashok's wife suddenly Sheela suffered a heart attack and all his happiness was shattered in one stroke.

The three sons came running after getting sad news. After all their rituals, everyone gathered in the evening at home.

The younger daughter-in-law raised the matter,

She: "Babuji, now how will you be able to stay here alone, you go with us."

Babuji: No daughter-in-law, let me stay here. There is a sense of living here in the children's household.

After this he said,

Babu Ji: Children, now your mother has left all of us. She has some things which You can share with each other.

Saying this he brought something out of the wardrobe.

The velvet bag had a very beautiful silver ornament having some jewelry, an old wristwatch made of gold. All of them jumped on so many beautiful things.

The elder son said in jest,

Elder son: Hey, this watch Amma wanted to give to Sarita. (Sarita was his wife)

Babuji: I have given you everything equally, so I want to give these two things to you three equally.

Everyone started looking at each other's faces. Then the middle son said with great hesitation,

Middle son: She used to talk to Meera about watch. Maybe she wanted to give this to Meera. (Meera was his wife)

But there was a problem. He was thinking in his mind that what should I give to the younger daughter-in-law.

Younger daughter-in-law: Babuji, probably you are thinking about me now. You should give the bag to Meera and the wristwatch to Sarita. Amma also wanted this.

Babuji: But Nandini, what should I give you. I don't understand.

She: You have one more precious thing and that Ammaji wanted to give it to me.

Everyone's eyes were open with surprise. Both daughters-in-law got very shocked. Now, which box will open! Sensing everyone's surprise and trouble, the younger daughter-in-law smiled and said,

She: You are the most precious, Babuji! Ammajihad told me last time that after her Babuji's care is mine. Just now you should follow her wish and go with us.

When children start sharing the responsibility with the property, they will stop being part of the family. Only the practice of sharing duties with rights can provide family coordination through equitable, flat.

And for sharing duties, the family is very important. Duties, relations is the thing which can make us happy by sharing these moments with our loved ones who are always with us.

So that Michael J. Fox said, **"Family is not an important thing. It's everything"**.

Chapter- 14 Connect to the world with Purpose

Discovering your purpose doesn't have to be complicated. Look at what you do and why you do it. Is it to support your family? That's your purpose. Is it to make a difference in your customer's life? That's your purpose. -Anne F. Beiler

This is true that everything in this universe is connected. But outer senses cannot see all the connections. The whole universe is a cosmic space of nothingness. It contains all bodies that exist in the cosmos. But the universe itself has nobody. It is pure nothingness. It is an alive presence that provides space to happen to everything. This alive prescience is called consciousness. Which is present within everyone as the center of their being. But we only catch physical and mental connections in our lives. If we can enter into our pure emptiness we will able to feel like inseparable parts of the whole. But since our mind gives us a limited image of ourselves which is ego, gives us the illusion that we are separate from the rest of the universe.

Even our physical body is not so limited as we think. The body that is with me now is part of the universe, but because we conceive of ourselves as ours, it becomes a problem: where does my body end?

If you go into it deeply, you will see that the whole universe is part of you, part of your body. For example, if the sun were to cease this very moment, your body could not continue to exist. It could not exist if there were no oceans, it could not exist if there were no atmosphere. Your body is just a part, a constantly changing part of the universe. When the sun rises, something rises in you. When the sun sets, something sets in you. When there is a moon, you are different. When there is no moon, you are different. Your body is in a constant, dynamic relationship with the whole.

Wherever you are, whatever state you are in, you will still be in a body. If your body is taken by the universe then the universe will give you another body, unless you consciously become the whole universe. Then there is no need for a body because the universe itself has nobody.

Individuals are bound to have bodies. But where does your body end and where does it begin? It is a problem, a multidimensional problem. Your body could not exist if your father's body had not been in existence. Your body is part of a long series, of an eternal series. Your body exists in the trees, in the sea, in everything. It is a small cosmos related to every part of the total.

You are swimming in the sea. You have left part of the sea behind and gone ahead, but the part that has been left behind is still a part of the sea in which you are now swimming. The sea is one and you are swimming in it just like the fish which is born of the sea and will dissolve into the sea. A fish is nothing but the sea itself, frozen somewhere, which will soon dissolve back into the sea again.

So it is a complex thing. But one thing is certain: nothing is dead. We are part of the ocean of life; we are aliveness. This universe is an infinite ocean of energy. Different bodies are frozen energies that look different from each other at the surface level. But all are part of the same ocean. All the difference exists on the surface level. The difference exists because our senses are limited and hence it cannot catch our connectivity with the whole.

It seems inconceivable to us because we go on seeing the universe from a particular point of view. That point is the disturbance. If that point dissolves and there is no ego to look from, then you cannot say that you are separate from the rest of the universe.

The connection is so powerful so that Metta World Peace said "For me, I saw a psychologist because I wanted to connect more with people, with the earth, my environment. I want to connect more to my family".

Chapter-15 Our Connection with Money

A bank is a place that will lend you money if you can prove that you don't need it. -Bob Hope

Why does a person who is already rolling in money want more? Think about how obsessed people can become with money, beyond its instrumental use, beyond rationality, beyond any easy explanation. Why does a person who is already rolling in money want more? Indeed, why do people whose lives are already comfortable making sacrifices in other areas of their lives – family, friendships and their own sanity – just to get more cash? Especially when, objectively, they appear to be rupees/dollars that they don't need.

Money is a by-product of success. Money can never be a direct measure of success. For example, earning money by doing something unethical or doing something you dislike is no measure of life satisfaction. Life satisfaction while paying the bills is a measure of success.

Of course, everyone needs enough money to pay the bills: food, housing, energy, communication, and transportation. Once you have enough money for those costs, your success is proportional to your ability to use your talents fully while satisfying a need in the real world.

The most common advice we hear is to save and do not overspend. Yes, they are important but just focus on saving, you won't be able to reach financial freedom and you will work 9 to 5 until you die.

If you earn Rs10,000/month, the maximum you can save is Rs.10,000/month assuming you still live with your parents and they cover all of your expenses.

Instead of just focusing on saving, focus on improving your skills/values so that you can generate larger income. Learn new skills to improve your values, read a lot of books about investment and start investing even if it starts small, start generating multiple income streams, and use leverages to reach your goals faster.

The key is to earn more, save, and invest. The more you earn, the more you can save and invest as long as you don't drastically change your spending habit. A lot of people spend a lot more and buy a bigger home when they earn more. Don't do this!

Chapter- 16 Our Connection with Health

Health is correlated with quality of life. If you get regular physical activity, have social connections, control your cholesterol, keep your blood pressure at a normal level, don't smoke - these things can make an enormous difference not only in how long you live, but how much you enjoy your life in those years.
-Tom Frieden

The connection is our interpretation of what we see and the impact it has on our emotions. This may be a perceptible influence or subconscious.

It's fairly widely accepted that how we think about things can, at some level, affect our physical well-being. To state it in the simplest terms, if what we see and experience causes us constant worry and anxiety, it can lead to stress which is known to be physically debilitating. On the flip side, interpreting what we see and experience in as positive a manner as possible can lead to better, more robust physical health. That's a very basic explanation, but one that has been proven out over time.

As I shared my story of a major breakdown in my health in 2017. I diagnosed with critical illness with no guaranty of life. but for my 7month baby I internally strongly decided to leave and dramatically I responded to treatment and recovered well and enjoying my fatherhood with my lovely daughter, celebrated her 4 birthdays successfully and hope to celebrate at least another 30 birthday of her with good health.

I experienced health is all about our internal state, we need to focus on emptyness within into internal world and build love to live and more importantly, consciously practice to enjoy life in every movement. miracles will happen in life and finally why we leave with fear, this life is very short so nothing is so serious in life. Be happy- No BP etc....

Chapter- 17 Grow as The Connector

"We all are so deeply interconnected; we have no option but to love all. Be kind and do good for any one and that will be reflected. The ripples of the kind heart are the highest blessings of the Universe."- Amit Ray

Connection is a bridge between human beings, we will not move forward in life without connection with another human being. Human connection is the exchange of positive energy between people. The potential of feeling understood and united through human connection is one of the most rewarding elements in life. It has the power to deepen the moment and the bond between people, inspire change and build trust.

Connecting with others is more important than you might think. Social connection can lower anxiety and depression, help us regulate our emotions, lead to higher self-esteem and empathy, and actually improve our immune systems.

From a neuroscience perspective, we are all connected brain to brain and cell to cell. By maintaining a self-awareness of our own thoughts, feelings and actions, we can choose to impact those around us, and thus our organizational culture, in very positive or negative ways.

Connection is the experience of oneness. It's having shared experiences, relatable feelings, or similar ideas. It is the feeling of belonging to something greater than oneself. When you're watching a sporting event with your friends, you're experiencing connection.

When people are connected emotionally, they share everything from their darkest secrets to deepest fears, and this builds trust and loyalty, having mutual respect is critical for a long-term relationship because when you respect your people, you value their dreams, feelings, and fears.